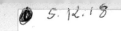

5.12.18

ᗺO

Please return/renew this item by the last date shown

worcestershire
countycouncil
Libraries & Learning

THE ONLY ONE FOR FRANK

Wartime, 1940. Frank is serving with the RAF, based at Montrose, where one bonny lass has caught his eye. Working in the local news-agent's shop, her name is Belle. When, happily, he's invited to her parents' home to meet Belle, his hopes soar — until he finds that she's already engaged to Jim. Then, unexpectedly, Belle breaks off her engagement. There's joy, tears, then happiness, amidst a world in tur-moil, as Frank and Belle begin their new life together . . .

JOAN CHRISTIE

THE ONLY ONE FOR FRANK

Complete and Unabridged

LINFORD
Leicester

First published in Great Britain in 2011

First Linford Edition
published 2011

British Library CIP Data

Christie, Joan.
   The only one for Frank.- -
   (Linford romance library)
   1. World War, *1939 – 1945*- -Social
   aspects- -Scotland- -Montrose- -Fiction.
   2. Love stories..
   3. Large type books.
   I. Title II. Series
   823.9'14–dc22

   ISBN 978–1–4448–0918–3

Published by
F. A. Thorpe (Publishing)
Anstey, Leicestershire

Set by Words & Graphics Ltd.
Anstey, Leicestershire
Printed and bound in Great Britain by
T. J. International Ltd., Padstow, Cornwall

This book is printed on acid-free paper

1

Every evening around 6pm, if he was off duty, Frank would stand at the entrance of one of the many closes up Montrose High Street. There, he would wait patiently to catch a glimpse of the lovely young woman who filled his dreams with her long, wavy dark hair, her slim figure and trim ankles. If only he could find a way of getting to know her.

He had been stationed with the RAF at Montrose aerodrome for a few months now and had first seen her three weeks before as he had been having a cigarette while idly looking in a shop window, when she had passed by. Smitten from that moment, he had since watched out for her and discovered she worked in a newsagents further up the street, hence his vigil when she finished work.

'Ach, Joe, I just canna stop thinking about her,' he'd confided in his pal with whom he had met up when they had been posted to this north-east town. 'If I could only find a way of knowing more about her. She's that bonny.'

'Aye lad, you've got it bad right enough,' replied Joe with a laugh. 'I hear you tossing and turning in your bed at night. Never mind, we're meeting up with Elsie and Freda later on. They're good company eh?'

So they sat drinking their beer in one of the town's pubs and thinking their own thoughts. Never far from their minds, besides beautiful young women, were thoughts of the war which was raging in Europe and Russia. It was March, 1940 and Frank had enlisted almost as soon as he had turned eighteen, which was two years before war broke out and he was now a lance-corporal. Elsie and Freda were two young Montrose girls they had met when they were home on leave from the WAAFs and, although they sometimes

2

made up a foursome for dances, walks or the pictures, they were just good friends.

Later that evening they walked the two nineteen year olds along the road from the dancehall, then stopped to speak before going on their separate ways, the men to their billets and the girls to their homes.

'We go back to Stafford on Monday lads,' confided Elsie. 'That's our leave up for another month or so.'

Joe bent down to give her a peck on the cheek.

'Ach, lassies, we'll miss your company. Will we see you afore you go?'

Elsie and Freda looked at each other and giggled, then nodded.

'We could go a walk round the Traill Drive if it's fine on Sunday after church,' suggested Freda and the men readily agreed.

The Traill Drive led round by the golf links and the picturesque beach and had been named after the man who paid for its construction. It was a walk which was popular with young and old alike. The links were wide, clear and bonny and the beach was a firm favourite in the summer months with its clean sands and the ebbing and flowing of the tides on its shores.

That night Frank was conscious of Joe lying in his nearby bunk and tried to keep his thoughts and body under control. Sighing, he pulled the blanket up over him and was soon in a deep sleep, knowing they'd be up with the lark to face another day of square bashing, making sure their equipment was up to scratch and seeing to the planes as they came back from sorties. Luckily he'd been brought up to work hard on his father's farm up in Banffshire and had no problems pulling his weight.

Sunday dawned bright and clear and, although the men could have worn civvies, they preferred to wear their smart airforce-blue uniforms and caps, thinking rightly that they made a better impression on the females.

Giving his shoes a final polish, Frank looked up at Joe who was squinting in the mirror on the inside of the clothes cupboard, one of which stood at the side of each bunk in the billet.

'Wonder if we'll ever get sent abroad, Joe lad?' Frank pondered.

'Don't even think about it,' his mate replied putting another dab of Brylcreem on his hair and combing his unruly curls as flat as he could. 'Who wants to leave this great wee toon and its bonnie lassies?'

Frank's thoughts turned again to the lass of his dreams. He certainly didn't want to leave here without first making contact with her. Every evening he had just followed her along the High Street into Murray Street then, when she turned to go down King Street, he'd stop and watch her until she was out of sight. If she'd had any inkling he was there, no doubt she would think he was some kind of weirdo and wouldn't want to get to know him.

'Come on dreamer,' Joe took hold of

his shoulder. 'Let's not waste our day off. Elsie and Freda will be waiting.'

Soon the two young men were striding along to the Drive where they had agreed to meet the girls.

'There they are,' said Joe. 'Don't they look right toffs in their Sunday best?'

The girls did indeed look smart. Elsie's coat was bright blue and she had a matching hat perched on her fair wavy hair while Freda favoured a green coat trimmed with ermine and also wore a close-fitting, matching hat and gloves.

'It's a bit breezy,' said Elsie, clutching her hat as they set off. Then the girls giggled as the young lads started marching and chanting,

'Left right, left right. I got a job for thirty bob, I got the sack and never went back. I left, left, left right, left.'

They joined in and other older couples smiled at them as they made their way along, a cheery sight, keeping thoughts of war at bay.

Soon they came to the Beach

Pavilion and, as usual, made their way past the attendant, up the stone steps inside, up to the balcony where they could look out over the beach, the links and the town.

'The steeple's impressive, isn't it?' remarked Frank looking to the west. 'Especially with the sun glinting on it like that.' He looked at Elsie who had come alongside him.

'Aye, we've a fine wee toon here,' she said. 'I've always liked biding here. I worked in Helen Carnegie's before the war,' she went on. 'It's the ladies' fashion shop in John Street. They said they'd keep my job open for after the war's over.'

'Ach, the war will be over soon, surely,' said Frank. 'It would suit you being in a dress shop — think o' a' the braw claes you could buy.'

'Huh, they'll a' be on coupons soon, but yes, it would be good to be back working there.'

She strolled over to the other side of the balcony then, as Frank turned, he saw her wave to someone coming along the esplanade. Joining her, he looked down casually then did a double-take. There she was — his dream-boat, linked in to another young woman and waving up to Elsie.

'You know her?' he croaked and cleared his throat. 'That young lady — you know her — the one with the grey suit?'

Elsie chuckled.

'I should do, she's my sister.'

'Your sister?' Frank almost choked then grabbed her shoulders. 'Could you — could you introduce us — please?'

Elsie looked up at him in amusement.

'Aye, if that'll please you. Come on.' Then she shouted over to their friends, 'Joe, Freda, we're going back down, see you in a mo'.' Then she grabbed Frank's hand and pulled him along beside her. They clattered down the stairs and out the entrance.

'Coo-ee, Belle. Over here. Someone wants to meet you.'

Belle — Frank's thoughts were in a whirl — didn't Belle mean beautiful in someone's language? Then, there she was in front of him, gazing up at him with her lovely green eyes. In a trance he clasped her hand and felt something like a shock go through him.

'Belle, this is Frank,' Elsie was saying. 'Frank, meet Belle, my older sister and this is . . . .' her voice trailed off and she looked bemused at the couple who seemed to be in another world. 'Frank,' she said giving him a shake. 'This is Daisy, Belle's pal.'

Frank tore his gaze reluctantly away and dutifully shook hands with Daisy, another fine looking woman but not a patch on Belle, his Belle, as he already thought of her. He frantically tried to think of a way to keep her here with him but the two women were already moving on although Belle did give him a backward glance as they said their goodbyes.

Turning back to Elsie, he gabbled, 'So she's your sister, your older sister.

That makes her what? Twenty, twenty-one?'

'She turned twenty-one in January.' Elsie looked at him curiously, then shrugged. 'Come on, let's get Freda and Joe and get on our way.' She looked up to where their friends were, still in the balcony and beckoned to them.

Frank's thoughts were in a whirl. His lovely lass, he now knew her name and that she was about a month older than himself AND that she was Elsie's sister, what an amazing coincidence, or fate, yes it had to be fate. He grasped Elsie's arm, alarming her somewhat.

'Elsie,' he said, 'You and Freda go back to Stafford tomorrow and, well, Joe and I will be gie lonely not knowing many folk here. Didn't you once say your parents made everyone welcome in their home?' He was scheming now, he knew, but needs must.

'Yes, yes, they do but . . . .' she was a bit suspicious of his motives with Frank now knowing Belle was her sister and he certainly seemed keen on her. Then,

10

making up her mind she said, 'Well, if you meet Belle from her work one night this week, she works in Isle's news-agents, you know, up at the Town House, about 6 o'clock, you might wrangle an invitation home.'

Frank could have hugged her. He never let on he already knew where Belle worked, he just said:

'Eh, could you perhaps drop a hint that I might be meeting her, that Joe and I are a bit lonely?'

Elsie nodded but, ah, she could see trouble ahead! But who was she to stand in anyone's way, didn't folk say all was fair in love and war?'

Then they joined up with their friends to continue their walk, each one deep in their own thoughts.

2

Frank, to his frustration, was on duty on Monday and Tuesday of the following week and he knew it was the shop's half-day closing on Wednesday so it was Thursday before he was finally back at his look-out point in the High Street close. He'd shared with Joe what he now knew about Belle and his pal had wished him well. Now he stood nervously twisting his cap in his hands and wondering how to approach her. Peeping out, just after 6pm, he saw her. She didn't swing her hips or shimmy down the street like some young women, but she walked with a purpose, like she was going somewhere. Well, if he had his way, it would be somewhere with him. Stubbing out his cigarette, he stepped out of the close and started up the street to meet her.

She looked neither left nor right and

he practically had to stand in front of her to get her attention.

'Well, hello Belle,' he managed to stammer. 'Remember we met on Sunday, with Elsie, your sister, round by the beach. I'm Frank.' And he stood and grinned stupidly at her. She looked bemused, then glanced at her watch, nodded and began to walk on.

Striding beside her and almost tripping over his own feet, he willed her to say something.

'Ah, yes, Frank,' she was smiling at him now and he uttered up a fervent prayer of thanks. 'Elsie did say you would maybe bump into me sometime. Look, I need to get home now but perhaps you and your friend would like to come up and meet Mum and Dad. Elsie told them about you. Perhaps on Sunday, you could come for tea?'

Frank stared at her, it was as simple as that. This Sunday, going to her house, meeting her parents, having tea together. It was bliss, it was heaven, it was all his dreams come together in one fell swoop. He felt like lifting her up in the air. Then he realised she was waiting for him to answer, with her head to one side and a curious look in her eyes.

'Yes. Eh, well now, that would be great. Joe and I, on Sunday, at your house. What, what time will we come?'

'Oh, about 3 o'clock would be fine. Now I must go, see you Sunday.' And she started off down the street again. He came to his senses and caught up with her.

'Just one thing,' he said sheepishly. 'Where do you live? Eh, what's your address?'

She laughed, a lovely gurgling sound.

'Of course. It's Carnegie Street, number 8, round the back of the close and up the stairs. The name Davis is on the door. Bye then.'

He stood and looked after her until she was out of sight then gave a whoop which made several people stop and smile. Then, just stopping himself from breaking into a run, he made his way back to the aerodrome whistling jauntily. Wait until he told Joe, he knew his pal would be glad for him and that they'd both been invited for tea. In just three days he would see her again, he could hardly wait.

As he expected, Joe had been delighted with the invitation and was glad for his friend that events seemed to be going his way. So it was that on the Sunday, they were once again making themselves presentable, this time for Belle and her parents.

'Has Belle any other sisters besides Elsie?' asked Joe as they made their way to Carnegie Street. 'Or brothers?'

'I've no idea,' replied Frank. 'Elsie never even mentioned Belle in all the weeks we've known her but we'll soon find out won't we?' And the two of them jostled and thumped each other playfully until they came to the close up which Belle lived.

'Here we go, pal. Will we pass muster, do you think?' said Frank, looking a bit anxious.

'Hey, if the Mum and Dad are as nice as their daughters are, by all accounts, we've no worries.'

They entered the close, made their way up the stairs and there, on the door, was the name Davis, just as Belle had said.

Frank rapped on the door and it was soon opened by Belle looking, to Frank's eyes, more beautiful than ever. She wore a close fitting, green woollen dress which came just past her knees and her dark hair was clipped back at the sides with Kirby-grips.

'Come in, Mum and Dad are waiting to meet you,' and she stood aside then ushered them into a living-room cum kitchen which was clean and cosy with a coal fire burning in the grate. Frank and Joe whipped off their caps and shook hands with Mr and Mrs Davis whose welcome was warm. Belle's mum was a small sparse woman whose permed hair was already turning grey and her eyes twinkled behind her spectacles showing intelligence. She was appraising the two young men and liked what she saw. Frank's attention was then drawn to Mr Davis who was at least 6 feet tall and stood straight and upright but it was his thatch of hair which was surprising. Although he had only been in his forties, his hair was as white as snow and they were to hear the tale behind it later.

'Sit down lads,' he said to them and pointed to the worn, brown leather settee which faced the fire. The two older people then sat themselves in the upright easy chairs at either side and Belle sat on one of the kitchen chairs between her Mum and Frank, whose heart was beating wildly. Then he remembered Belle and Joe hadn't been introduced and, amidst laughter, they too shook hands. They all chatted away about where the lads came from and their families. Then Mrs Davis pointed to three portraits above the fireplace.

'That's Elsie in her uniform,' she said proudly, 'and our two sons, Bert and Sam in theirs. We've just Belle at home now and hope she won't take it into her head to join up too.'

Belle laughed and shook her head.

'Not unless I have to Mam. Now boys, would you like a cup of tea before we have our proper tea at about 5 o'clock?'

'Thank you,' said Frank and Joe in unison and their eyes followed Belle as she got up gracefully and filled the kettle at the sink before putting it on the gas cooker which she lit with a taper from the fire.

They had a fine cuppie and home-made rock buns which Belle admitted to making the night before and which Frank declared as being 'just right'. He would have enjoyed them if they had tasted like sawdust because 'his' Belle had made them. Then, at Mr Davis's suggestion, they all had a game of whist round the wooden kitchen table and which Joe won amidst much hilarity.

Afterwards they all helped with setting the table and sat round it while Belle dished up delicious mince, tatties and vegetables which had been boiling away on the cooker and which they all enjoyed.

'By, that was braw,' said Joe after mopping up the gravy with a slice of bread. 'Reminds me of home.'

'We're so grateful,' added Frank, nodding his appreciation.

Belle and her Mum then donned their pinnys and, telling the men to sit and enjoy their smoke, they set to wash and dry the dishes.

'What do you work at?' asked Frank of Mr Davis, realising the older man was too old to be called up but still wondering about his white hair.

'Well lad, I was in the Home Guard during the 1st World War but I've worked on the railways since. I'm a ganger on the tracks and like it weel enough but was aince in a nasty accident, hence my white hair.'

Intrigued, Frank and Joe nodded their encouragement for him to go on.

'Weel, I was working away, down at the cutting and must have been dreaming a bit and didn't hear a train coming. One of the other men shouted a warning and I jumped off the track but the train caught me a blow and I was sent flying. Unconscious I was. They took me to the Infirmary and I was swathed in bandages with all my injuries, including to my head. When they took off the bandages my hair had turned from black to pure white. Over ten years ago, it was.'

Belle and her Mum had finished the dishes and joined them.

'Aye,' said Belle quietly. 'I hardly mind Dad's hair being any other than white.'

They all sat in silence for a few minutes then were startled by a loud knocking at the door.

'Ah, that'll be Jim,' said Belle jumping up and going quickly to the door.

Mrs Davis sat looking at Frank and wondered how things were going to go now. She'd seen the way he looked at Belle.

A tall, rather bumptious looking man appeared in the doorway.

'Frank, Joe,' said Belle. 'I'd like you to meet Jim, my fiancé.'

As Frank's heart fell to the soles of his boots, he noticed the ring on her finger for the first time.

3

Frank sat, his head in his hands, on his bed in the billet and groaned.

'Why didn't I notice the ring before, was I blind? And why didn't I guess she'd be spoken for, a lovely young lass like her? What do I do now?'

After being introduced to Belle's fiancé, who Frank felt like giving a wallop on the chin, he and Joe had hastily taken their leave. They thanked Mr and Mrs Davis and, when the older woman had said 'Haste ye back,' they had mumbled something and made for the door.

Belle seemed a bit bewildered but had come out with them and stood at the top of the stairs as they had stumbled down them.

'You've been good company,' she said hesitatingly. 'Perhaps we'll see you again.'

Frank gave her a forlorn backward glance. Before, he would have jumped at the chance, but he now wanted to get away and lick his wounds. They bid her goodbye and fled and were now back at the aerodrome.

'Frank, lad,' said Joe, standing over his chum. 'If you're really keen on Belle, and I'm sure you are, dinna gie up so easily. Aren't you always telling me that if something's worthwhile, then go for it and Belle's worthwhile isn't she? Worth fighting for?'

Frank looked up, his trusting brown eyes searching his pal's face, looking for answers, for hope.

'Aye Joe, I ken you're right. It's just going to take some getting used to. I mean, how do I approach the problem now? I can't very well meet her from work again, can I? And I couldn't face going back to her Mum and Dad's knowing she'll be there and isn't available. He seemed an arrogant looking bloke too, did you no' think? Not good enough for her anyhow. I could have thumped him one.'

'Huh. That would have put you in her good books too, wouldn't it? Look, we've got to think of a plan, a strategy. Isn't that what our officers are always telling us?'

'A plan, aye — how to get rid of the enemy. And just how do we go about that, may I ask?'

'Well, first we find out about him. He was wearing civvies, he's not with our lot, so he's in the army or the navy or, hah, maybe he's a conchie. If so he should be easy to get rid of, in the nicest possible way, of course.'

'A conscientious objector — oh Joe, I hardly think Belle would . . . . . . Well, who knows? Anyway how do we find out about him and get to know Belle better? Tell me that.'

Joe looked thoughtful.

'Leave it to me, old chum. I've just thought of a way.' Then, as Frank looked at him expectantly went on. 'Trust me, never fear, Joe is here. Now, let's have a game of cards then some shut-eye. We're on duty early tomorrow and we can drown our sorrows at the pub later on.'

Frank rather morosely agreed and, that night, in bed, his dreams were, once more, filled with Belle but this time, a large menacing figure was in the background and he awoke restless and sweating. How he hoped Joe's plan, whatever it was, would work.

Later that week, Joe came bursting into the billet and, ignoring the other men, strode up to where Frank was playing a game of patience with the pack of cards.

'Didn't I tell you I'd think of something? Eh? Didn't your old pal manage to find a way?' He prodded Frank who grinned half-heartedly at him.

'A way to what?' he asked wearily.

'To find a way to your lady love's heart, that's what. Move over and I'll tell you.'

Frank showed a flicker of interest and dutifully moved along the bunk to let his friend sit down.

'Well?'

'Well, I went to see Belle's Mum today, didn't I?'

'What! Whatever did you say to her?'

'Oh, I just said I'd called to get Elsie and Freda's address at their camp in England.'

'Huh. What good will that do?'

'Well, she asked me in for a cup of tea and we got chatting. Turns out Jim, the fiancé, was turned down by the army because he has flat feet and a bad chest.'

'Ho, ho. Oh well, but that didn't stop Belle getting engaged to him, did it?'

'No, no lad. And his Dad's got a tripe shop in the High Street. That's where Jim works.'

Frank almost choked at that.

'A tripe shop. Oh lad, it would be funny if it wasn't so serious. So where does that leave me?'

'Well, Mrs Davis likes you, she said as much, and she's not too keen on Jim, thinks he wangled his way into Belle's affections. Anyway, I got the lassies' address, we can write to them and Elsie can drop a few hints to Belle about how you feel. Take it from there, eh?'

So Frank and Joe duly wrote to Elsie and Freda, but before the girls had a chance to reply, fate once again stepped in.

Frank just happened to be walking along Montrose High Street at about 6 o'clock one evening the following week, although he'd given up lurking in closes, and Belle came walking towards him. They both stopped and smiled then spoke simultaneously:

'How are you?' then they both laughed.

'You first,' said Frank drowning in her green eyes.

'Well, I'm fine,' replied Belle, 'but Mam's a bit poorly. I feel awful being out at work as is Dad and she's on her own during the day apart from a neighbour who looks in. It's her bronchitis, she takes it badly every so often.'

'Oh, I'm sorry,' said Frank, then, seizing the opportunity went on, 'How would it be if I looked in to see her one day? Would she mind?'

'I'm sure she'd be pleased. She'll be on her own tomorrow morning until Dad and I get home at lunchtime, but perhaps you're on duty?'

'No, no. As it happens I'm off until later in the day. Can I take her anything?'

'Your company would be enough, though you could perhaps make her a cup of tea.'

'Certainly, I'll do that and anything else she needs.'

'Thank you eh, Frank. I'll have to get home now to put on the tea, they'll be waiting. It's so good of you. Bye.'

'It's a pleasure,' said Frank to her retreating back then, whistling once again, crossed the street for it wouldn't do to follow her again, and made his way back to the aerodrome with a lighter heart than he'd had all week.

Next morning Frank was up with the

lark and, as usual, had to be on parade early with the rest of the men then, after drill and inspection, was able to go back to his billet to ready himself for his visit to Mrs Davis. Joe was on duty, otherwise he might have gone with him but he was pleased to have the chance to be on his own with Belle's Mum, poorly or not.

By 10 o'clock he was knocking on the door of the house which Joe and himself had left so abruptly the Sunday before. Realising that she might be too ill to answer the door, he opened it and shouted:

'Coo-ee Mrs Davis, it's me, Frank.'

He heard a rather hoarse call from the kitchen cum living-room and went in to find her sitting in her armchair in front of the fire with a shawl round her shoulders and her feet on a stool. She gave him a sweet smile and, her eyes twinkling, beckoned him to the other armchair. Before he sat down he noticed that the coal-scuttle was nearly empty and the fire was getting low.

'Will I fetch more coal, Mrs Davis?' he asked kindly and she nodded and pointed downstairs.

'Coal-cellar in the close,' she croaked and he remembered seeing the row of doors lining the close outside.

'I'll just be a tick,' he said and picked up the coal-scuttle and shovel and went out to return 5 minutes later with it full.

'Not too much,' she said, as he made to put more coal on the fire. 'Have to be careful.'

He knew she meant economically as well as for safety and put on just enough to send out a cheery warmth into the room.

'Now, a cup of tea?' he asked and she nodded gratefully.

Soon the two of them were sitting companionably sipping their hot sweet tea and eating a digestive biscuit which he'd been told to find in a tin in the sideboard.

'Belle's a good lass,' she said watching him carefully. She was a shrewd woman and, as Joe had said, wasn't all that taken with Belle's fiancé, Jim, but had liked Frank on sight and it hadn't escaped her notice the way he'd looked at her.

Frank's eyes lit up as he agreed that she was, indeed, a good lass.

'And a bonnie one too, Mrs Davis. Truth to tell I'm fair smitten and was a bit taken aback to find she was engaged.'

Her 'humph' at that said it all.

'She'll be at the dancing on Saturday night,' she confided. 'The Angus Hall.'

'Ah, well,' said Frank sighing. 'But Jim'll be there, no doubt and, well, I've two left feet.'

'Laddie,' she reached over and patted his hand. 'Even that's better than two flat feet.'

They looked at each other, then both started chuckling which sent her into a paroxysm of coughing and she had to motion to him for her cough medicine on the sink. He measured out a spoonful for her and she swallowed it down like a child.

He took his leave of her shortly afterwards but her words came back to him as he made his way to the aerodrome in time to go on duty. Only two words but they filled him with hope.

'You'll do,' she had said and clasped his hand in her tiny one before she sat back in her chair and closed her eyes, for the time being, quite exhausted.

4

The day following Frank's visit to Belle's Mum, he had a letter from Elsie. In it, she told him of the boredom of being at the camp in Stafford although they were kept busy enough. Tedious was the word she used and Frank could empathise with that as he and Joe felt the same way. Although there was a war going on and they had to be prepared for any eventuality, they weren't actually in the thick of it being so far away from any action.

Elsie then went on to say much the same as Joe had done — that if Frank was serious about Belle, he wouldn't let anything stand in his way, unless, of course, Belle wasn't interested. Wishing him and Joe all the best, she said she hoped her and Freda would see them the next time they were home on leave. Then there was a P.S. at the bottom of the letter saying that she would write and drop a few hints to her sister about the way Frank felt about her. He showed Joe the letter later when they had their dinner in the canteen.

'What's the next stop then pal?' he asked Joe.

'Well, didn't Mrs Davis tell you that Belle would be at the dance on Saturday? We could go along, you ask her up to dance and I guess you'll be able to gauge if there's any magnetism between you as you hold her in your arms. Eh, old chum?'

Frank laughed. 'I suppose you're right. And with this blooming war we'll never know when we'll be posted so the sooner I make a move the better, eh?'

'That's the stuff. You show her you're the man of her dreams, not old flat feet — she'll be swooning in your arms with all of your charms and the next thing you know you'll be married with a brood of bairns to keep you out of mischief.'

'Steady on, lad. I'm not over the first

hurdle yet. As for a brood of bairns, I want family of course, after all, my Mum and Dad had ten of us, so I'm used to that but first — how am I to learn to dance before Saturday?'

'Wait until it's a slow foxtrot, even you could manage that without treading on toes, surely. Just relax, forget about your feet and concentrate on your feelings. Now, let's have some more of that jam roly-poly before it's all done. It's filling up a corner of my stomach nicely and it's a while till tea-time.'

They then spent the rest of the afternoon stripping the engine of one of the jeeps, tinkering with it and oiling the parts but their thoughts were on Saturday's dance and the young women they hoped to dance with or, in Frank's case, the one woman who filled his thoughts.

Saturday soon came round and they made their way to the Angus Hall in the centre of the town. They had a wee dram at one of the pubs first to give them Dutch courage and were both in a happy mood as they entered the hall. Frank quickly scanned the crowd of young folk, most of the men in uniform, but saw no sign of Belle or her fiancé.

He and Joe lit up their cigarettes and enjoyed watching the dancers do the quicksteps, foxtrots, polkas, tangos and Gay Gordons but Frank kept one eye on the door looking out for 'his' girl. He was just beginning to despair of her showing up, when she entered with Jim at her side. She was as lovely as ever with a powder blue dress which was calf-length and had a sweetheart neckline. He thought of the corny phrase 'their eyes met across the crowded room' but that is just what happened.

Joe had spoken about magnetism when he'd dance with her, but it was there in their glance. As she recognised him, she smiled and, taking Jim's arm, came across to where they stood.

'Hello again,' she said. 'Jim, you've met Frank and Joe, remember?'

All Jim did was give a grunt as he

glowered at them and Frank, once again, wondered what Belle saw in him. Without stopping to think, he stammered,

'Would you like to dance, Belle?' and his heart leapt as she accepted. Then he realised his mistake — it was a quickstep and he felt foolish as he tried to manoeuvre her round the room. After treading on her toes a few times, he suggested they sit this one out and she readily agreed. As Joe and Jim joined them, he then asked if they would like tea or lemonade which was on sale in a corner of the room. They all agreed lemonade would be fine and he thankfully escaped to fetch four glasses for them. Balancing them on a tray, he returned and, as they got a table and sat sipping, Belle laid a hand on his arm.

'Frank, I want to thank you for being with Mam the other day. She enjoyed your company and is feeling better today.'

Frank felt pleased and, as their eyes met and caught, her green eyes gazed into his brown ones and Joe and Jim were forgotten as was everyone else in the room. Nothing, just nothing, would stop Frank making Belle his girl, he thought, then was brought back to reality as smoke was blown right into his face. Startled he looked round at Jim and saw the hostility in the other man's face as he ground out his cigarette.

'Come on, Belle, it's time we were going,' he growled, gripping her arm.

'Already Jim? But we're just here. Can't we stay just a little while?'

'I don't think so. Get your coat. The air in here is making me choke.'

Belle looked unhappy but dutifully slipped on her coat, then Jim took her arm and ushered her out.

Joe and Frank looked at each other in disbelief but, before they could speak, Jim came back and thrust his face menacingly into Frank's.

'Belle's my girl — don't you forget it or you'll be sorry,' he muttered then left abruptly.

'The man's a maniac,' said Joe. 'Come on Frank, let's go and get a drink before the pubs shut. I think you need one.'

Frank felt cut up by Jim's behaviour and the fact that Belle was engaged to such an unpleasant character. But what could he do? And had Jim been threatening him? He just had to see Belle on her own, he knew she was attracted to him, it showed in her eyes. But there was nothing he could do right then so he joined his chum as they went off to forget their worries, albeit temporarily, with a drink.

5

After Jim and Belle left the dance-hall, Jim gripped his fiancee's arm and steered her along towards her home.

'Jim, stop, you're hurting me,' Belle said, trying to free herself. 'What's got into you, stop it now.'

Jim just gripped her harder and continued to hurry her along. All too soon they reached Carnegie Street. He stopped abruptly and turned her to face him.

'You're my girl, don't forget it. I saw the way you looked at that RAF bloke. They think they're God's gift to women in their uniforms. The sooner they're sent abroad the better. Now, I'll see you on Wednesday — we'll go to the pictures and I expect you to stay in and do your knitting in the evenings till then. Alright?'

Belle just stared at him, trembling a

little at this side to the man which she hadn't come across before. He leant down and gave her a brusque peck on the cheek, turned on his heel and stormed off.

Shakily, she made her way up the stairs and into the house where her Mum and Dad were sitting contentedly by the fireside. Mrs Davis looked up and smiled at her daughter then, with her usual keen perception, noticed all was not well.

'You're home early Belle,' she said. 'Is everything alright?'

Belle tried to compose herself but went through to her bedroom to remove her coat without saying anything which caused her parents to glance at each other questioningly. Coming back through, Belle smoothed down her dress, then, as she saw the love and concern in her parents' eyes, her composure gave way and she sat down with a thump on the sofa.

'No Mam, actually things aren't alright at all. We met Frank and Joe at the dance and Jim turned nasty. He said we were leaving when we'd barely got there and he practically dragged me home. I don't know what got into him . . . . well, I do really. It seems he's jealous of Frank but I hardly know him. He's very nice and attentive and he was so good coming to see you Mam but there was no need for Jim to act like that.'

There was silence then Mr Davis, a placid, gentle man, got up and went to fill the kettle while his wife reached across and took Belle's hand.

'Oh, lass, I don't know what to say. You said you hardly know Frank but, well do you really know Jim? After all you were only going out with him for a few months when he proposed and he didn't even ask your Dad first, did he?'

Belle looked thoughtfully at her Mum and shook her head.

'No, Mam, he didn't. I suppose he thought because I was nearly twenty-one at the time, he didn't have to and, after tonight, I just wonder if I know him well at all. He was really horrible. Jealousy is a terrible thing but he's nothing to be jealous of, does he, Mam?'

'Well lass, as you say, you hardly know Frank but he seems a decent chap. Who knows? He's sweet on you anyway.' Then, as Belle's eyes opened wide with surprise, she went on, 'Here's Dad, made a cup of tea for us. You'll feel better after that and an early night. Things will look better in the morning.'

But, as Belle lay unsleeping in her bed later, her thoughts were on the coming Wednesday and seeing Jim again. Did she really want to face him after tonight? And what right did he have telling her to stay in and 'do her knitting'? Jealous, domineering, possessive . . . . what other traits did he have that she didn't know about? Then she remembered looking into Frank's eyes and how she'd felt as she did so.

Perhaps Jim did have reason to be jealous. Oh, bother, why did life have to be so complicated all of a sudden? What was going to happen next, she wondered before she finally drifted off to sleep.

Frank and Joe, after a restless night, due mainly to Jim's behaviour but also to the amount of drink they had consumed afterwards, were rudely awakened at an unearthly hour by their sergeant bellowing for them to 'get up sharp and be on parade at six hundred hours.' Feeling deathly, they stumbled around showering, shaving and dressing as smartly as they could and wondering what it was all about. Soon they were lined up with the other men and it didn't help that there was a steady drizzle falling on them and the morning was a bit chilly. They soon found out what it was all about. Later they sat on their beds disconsolately.

'I don't believe it,' moaned Frank. 'We've just settled in here nicely. I've fallen for a beautiful woman who I mean to marry and we're told we're getting moved on. To Chester of all places, Chester, England, and not next month, not next week but tomorrow. Oh no, Joe.'

'It's not abroad anyway, pal. We've that to be thankful for. And we'll get leave. You can come back up here if you really want to.'

'Want to!' exclaimed Frank. 'Of course I want to. Look, I've got to see Belle. We've a lot to do before we move out but I'm going to nip into town at dinner-time, go to her house, her Mum will be there, she'll understand. I'll ask Belle if she'll meet me tonight. I've just got to see her on her own, see if she's really serious about that Jim. He's such a creep, Joe.'

'Yes Frank, he certainly seems to be. Now, come on, we'll have to get a move on. If you want off for a couple of hours tonight, we'll have to buckle down now. Just be thankful you've met someone you care so much about.'

'You're right, Joe and somehow I feel it in my bones that it'll turn out okay. It's just hard to take the way things are going just now. Could be worse though, she could be married to him. Now come on — all systems go.'

Dinner-time saw Frank skipping his meal and going to Belle's house, his heart in his mouth. Soon he was knocking at the door and, when Mrs Davis opened it, he hastily explained that his unit was moving on next day and he needed to talk to Belle. She welcomed him in, sat him down and quietly told him about Jim's behaviour the night before. Frank clenched and unclenched his fists at the thought of Belle being treated badly then readily agreed, when Belle arrived, to having a plate of soup with them. Belle couldn't help but show her delight in him being there which gladdened his heart and her face fell when he repeated about moving on. Frank then asked if he could see her that evening.

He and Mrs Davis looked anxiously at Belle as they waited for her reply. Then they both laughed in relief as Belle nodded and said;

'Yes, I'll see you Frank as you're

going away but, well, I am engaged so perhaps you could come here and we could just talk if that's okay.'

Frank agreed and then, seeing the time on the mantelpiece clock, got to his feet and arranged to arrive back at 6 o'clock. He took Belle's hand in his and they looked deeply into each other's eyes once more. He had to drag himself away but knew he'd be in trouble if he didn't get back to the aerodrome.

'See you soon,' he said simply then hurried off rejoicing that he'd be with her again before long and that, unless he was very much mistaken, she felt as much for him as he did for her.

Although there was so much to do that afternoon, it seemed to drag for Frank but, luckily, his sergeant understood and gave him a couple of hours off that evening. In fact, many of the men requested time off and this was granted on the proviso that they were back at the 'drome by 9 o'clock as the convoy was moving out early the next morning. They were also warned not to have too much to drink.

At 6 o'clock precisely, he was back at Belle's but, of course, she was just returning from her work and he waited patiently with a cup of tea while she had her meal. By the time this was over and she had helped her Mum with the dishes, he was counting the minutes he'd have left with her. To his surprise, however, Belle's Mum declared she needed the kitchen table to cut out a dress pattern and they would have to go through to the front parlour for their chin-wag. Frank followed Belle through.

'What's Mam been up to?' declared Belle. 'The fire's lit, first time for ages in this room. Well, it's cosy anyway. Sit down, Frank.'

Frank inwardly blessed Mrs Davis for her foresight but noticed the sofa was avoided as Belle sat down in an easy chair and he took the other. They sat in silence for a few awkward moments then Frank noticed the budgie in its cage in a corner of the room.'

'Ah, a budgie,' he said, getting up and going over to peer in at the green bird. 'What's it's name?'

'Billy's a pretty boy,' twittered the pet, right on cue and they both laughed. The ice was broken and they were soon chatting. Frank told Belle about his six brothers and three sisters, some of them in the forces but three of his older brothers worked on farms and were exempt and the younger ones were still at school. He also explained his Dad had been in an accident some years before and was no longer able to work but that his Mum had taken over a boarding house and tea-rooms in Banff which was popular with those in the forces on leave and also with the police force for meals.

'A busy life then, Frank,' said Belle. 'You'll be used to hard work.'

'Yes,' said Frank. 'Mum brought us all up to do our bit and we also had to go to church every Sunday.'

Belle looked thoughtfully at the

young man opposite, taking in his neat dark hair, honest brown eyes, his cheery grin and the endearing dimple in his chin. She suddenly realised she'd been staring and he was looking intently at her. A bit embarrassed, she looked down at her hands and twiddled with her engagement ring. Frank got up and, going over to her, took her hands in his.

'Belle,' he began, clearing his throat, 'You must know how I feel about you. Is, is there any chance . . . .?' his voice tailed away.

'Oh, Frank, don't, please. I can't — I mean, I'm engaged to Jim. I can't just . . . .'

'Belle, your Mum told me about his behaviour last night. Does that sound like a loving man, a kind man?'

'No, but it was so unlike him. I don't know, I do like you but, oh Frank, I think you'd better go before it gets more complicated, please.'

Frank stood up and let go of her hands. Then he remembered Joe's words and Elsie's — if he was really serious, he'd fight for her.

'Okay, Belle, I'll go now, but I'm not giving you up. I haven't known you long but I've never felt like this for anyone before. And, no matter if you're denying it, there's chemistry between us — I know it. Please just write to me and I'll come back as soon as I get leave again. And watch out for that Jim — be careful, eh?'

'Yes, Frank.' Belle's voice was just a whisper. 'Take care of yourself, won't you?' With that Frank had to be content then, after giving her a gentle kiss on the cheek, he went through to her parents and wished them goodnight. As Mrs Davis came to the door with him, he could, to his surprise, just hear the tinkling of Some Enchanted Evening being played on the piano in the front room. The tune was to linger in his memory for the next few months with thoughts of Belle always uppermost in his mind, which kept him going through these dark days of war which kept on raging.

Belle didn't write but Elsie did and he even had a letter from Mrs. Davis wishing him and Joe well and saying that Jim and Belle were still going out together but that Jim was as surly as ever and Belle had withdrawn into herself a bit. She ended by saying that he'd be most welcome at their home when he got leave though she knew he'd want to visit his own folk up north also.

This was indeed a quandary for Frank but then something unexpected happened one hot July day just before he was due for some leave. Something which made his mind up that his folks could wait a wee while but to see Belle couldn't.

6

It was now the month of July month
and Frank wiped the sweat from his
brow as he tinkered with the engine of
one of the jeeps. The weather had gone
from relentless rain to being hot and
sultry and he stopped working for a
minute to take a slug of water from the
bottle at his feet. Then, to his surprise, a
corporal came over to him with a broad
grin on his face.

'You're wanted in Herbie's office,
pronto Frank. I'll take over here.'

Herbie was the Flight Sergeant's
nickname and Frank wondered what he
was wanted for. Musing over possibili-
ties but coming up with nothing
concrete, he thanked his fellow corporal
(he'd had promotion just weeks before)
and made his way to the office.
Knocking sharply on the door and
straightening his shoulders, he heard

the order to enter. Seeing Herbie at his desk, he was surprised to see that he too had a grin on his face.

'Ah, Corporal Pirie, I think you would agree that you have worked hard since you joined the RAF, earned your stripes and all that. Deserve a wee break, do you think?'

Frank could only stare and stutter his agreements, wondering what it was all about.

'Well, eh, if you go through to my back office, you'll find someone who will escort you into town for the afternoon. Be back here at 6 o'clock sharp though, do you hear?'

Mystified Frank nodded, then as Herbie flung open the inner door, he gasped when he saw standing there in her WAAF's uniform and smiling at him, none other than Elsie.

If it couldn't be Belle, the next best person to lift him out of the doldrums was her sister. Grasping her hand in his and controlling himself not to hug her in front of the Officer, his brown eyes shone with delight and welcome.

'Elsie, whatever are you doing here? You're quite a bit from Stafford. Don't say you're getting billeted here?'

'No Frank. But your Flight Sergeant says you can take a jeep and drive us into town. I'll explain over a cup of tea if we can find a café.'

Hardly believing this turn of events and that he'd hear first hand news of Belle, Frank explained that he'd just give himself a wash and tidy up if she'd wait ten minutes for him. She readily agreed and soon they were speeding into nearby Chester and chatting nineteen to the dozen.

'One of my chums in the WAAF has a sister in Chester and got two days leave to visit her. When I heard about it, I begged her to take me. She was happy for me to come along and also for me to stay with her sister so . . . . here I am.'

Frank glanced at her and felt his heart lurch, she was so like Belle. Then they both laughed happily and drove the rest of the way in companionable silence until they reached the picturesque town with its clock tower landmark.

'It's only 2 o'clock,' said Frank. 'We'll have a cuppie and catch up on news, then have a walk and there should be time for a meal before I have to get back. How's that?'

'Sounds perfect,' agreed Elsie. 'It's so hot though. I'll have to take off my uniform jacket and hat. What about you?'

'Couldn't agree more,' Frank said as he went round the side of the jeep and helped Elsie down. They were parked in the town's square and noticed a small café opposite. Each divested of their jackets and hats, then made their way over and were relieved that, with both the front and back doors of the café open and an extractor fan whirring from the ceiling, the interior was blessedly cool.

'I feel more like a pint of beer than a

cup of tea,' said Frank, 'but it wouldn't do taking you to a pub even if they were open. I guess it's enough that you're here and we have the afternoon free.'

The café was quite busy with both civilians and other men in uniform but they secured a table near one of the doors. When a young lass in a neat black skirt and white blouse with a frilly apron came over for their order, they settled for a pot of tea and a couple of scones.

'It's so good to see you,' said Frank, reaching for Elsie's hand once they had been served. 'How are your Mum and Dad?'

'They're just fine,' replied Elsie. 'Mam is keeping better in this good weather and Dad's working away as usual. He comes off on holiday next week and they're having a couple of days visiting my Granny in Brechin and Mam's sisters..'

'And . . . .Belle,' said Frank falteringly, 'she's doing okay is she?'

'We-ll, yes. She's okay but . . . .'

'But? But what, Elsie?'

'Look Frank, I've some news for you about Belle. But let's have this tea and bite to eat, then I'll tell you when we find a sheltered place on our walk, where we can talk in private.'

Frank had to contain his frustration at not knowing what Elsie had to say but he manfully ate his scone and drank his tea as they made small talk. Soon though they were out in the sunshine once more and making their way along a lane where they found a bench which was thankfully shaded by a large oak tree. Slinging their jackets and caps alongside them, they sat together and Frank turned to Elsie.

'Right lass, you said Belle's okay, then you said but . . . . What is it? What is the but . . . .?'

He hoped with all his heart that his sweetheart hadn't gone and married that bounder. No, surely not. Yet she hadn't written once in the ten weeks he'd been back at the camp and he'd agonised over that. But, what was Elsie saying?

'Jim got called up after all, Frank. The powers-that-be decided they need all the men and women they can muster even if they have handicaps. He's been given an office job in the army and I think he's somewhere in England.'

Frank breathed a sigh of relief.

'But you surely know where he is, Elsie. And how is Belle taking it?'

'Well, that's the other thing. When Jim broke the news to her that he had been called up, she decided that, because of his possessiveness and nastiness, she no longer loved him, if indeed she ever did and . . . .'

And, Elsie?' Frank could have shaken the young woman beside him with impatience.

'And Belle's broken off their engagement. His behaviour when she did was such that she's glad she's seen the back of him. She's sad it had to happen but she's more like her old self again. She said it was like being out with a powder keg when they went out together.'

Elsie broke off as she looked at Frank. He was positively beaming and, indeed, it took him all his will-power not to shout out in delight.

'Oh, Elsie, lass. You don't know how happy that's made me feel. It's like a great weight's been taken off me. Do you think there's a chance for me with Belle?'

'I think you know that yourself, Frank. The way's clear for you to make a move now and Mam's always got an open door for you. You can't, of course, actually stay at our house, but Mam's neighbours, the Thomsons, at number six, would give you a bed for the night if you got leave.'

'You bet I can. I'm due some anyway 'cause I've been working hard and fore-going any leave I could have had. It was my way of dealing with the situation. Has Belle any holidays coming up?'

'Hadn't you better ask her yourself? I'm sure she'd love to get a letter from you and well . . . . you can take it from there.'

The rest of the day passed in a daze for Frank. He and Elsie spoke some more, went a pleasant walk then had a meal in a small hotel, but all Frank's thoughts were on Belle and their possible future together. After seeing Elsie safely to the door of her friend's sister's house, he sped happily back to the aerodrome where he quickly sought out his old pal, Joe.

After relating this wonderful news to him, Joe patted his shoulder and said quietly,

'Oh, lad, I'm that glad for you. I was getting worried about you, working all the time but now . . . . well, didn't you say a while back that you felt it would all turn out alright?'

Frank lay back on his bunk, his hands behind his head and sighed happily. Tomorrow, he'd write to Belle, arrange leave and then . . . . well, there'd be no stopping him.

7

So it was that, after having written to Belle and having had a short note in return arranging for him to stay with their neighbours, Frank got a long weekend pass for the beginning of August and was soon on his way north.

He could hardly wait for the train to reach Montrose and, when it did, he was delighted to see Mr Davis in his railwayman's uniform, waiting on the platform.

'Ah, lad you made it then,' he welcomed Frank and shook his hand as he alighted from the train. 'Belle's working today but is off the rest of the weekend. Her Mum has dinner ready for you and you know the way.'

'Thanks, Mr Davis. I see you're back at work after your ain holiday. Have a fine time did you?'

'Ach, it was ower hot in July. It's just

fine now though. Weel I'll hae tae get back on the line, the men will be waiting. I'll see you at teatime.'

'That'll be grand,' responded Frank. 'Bye just now then.'

Then Frank went striding out of the station so glad to be back in Montrose that he whistled cheerily all the way to Carnegie Street. Many a housewife or young lass smiled at the sight of him, so handsome in his uniform. It fairly cheered them up.

Soon he was climbing the stairs to the familiar green painted door with Davis on the brass nameplate. He hardly had time to knock when Belle's Mum opened the door and reached up to give him a welcome hug and a peck on his cheek.

'Oh, laddie, you're a sight for sair eyes. Come on in. Belle will be home shortly and we'll have our dinner.'

He followed her into the kitchen where the coal fire was burning despite the heat of the day. It was like coming home for him and seeing the neat sparse wee body clad in her wrap-around apron and the usual twinkle in her eyes, fairly warmed his heart.

They sat and chatted for a while then the door opened and there she was, his Belle, looking as lovely as ever. Standing up, he strode over to her and put his arms tentatively round her momentarily. Her scent, the Evening in Paris which she always wore, made him almost giddy.

After their dinner of roast beef, tatties and vegetables, Belle shyly took her leave to return to work. Frank was happy with the knowledge that she'd be back after 6 o'clock and they'd have the weekend together.

'Come away then, Frank,' said Mrs Davis. 'Bring your bag and we'll go downstairs to Mrs Thomson where you'll be sleeping. She has two sons in the army and you're to have their room. You'll eat with us and can come and go as you like.'

So the afternoon passed with Frank meeting the widowed neighbour, seeing the room. Then, once back upstairs, he helped Belle's Mum with the dishes and afterwards, made himself useful.

'Well, lad, if you want something to do,' said the older woman, 'there's the grass to cut. It gets a bit much for Father, it grows so quickly in this heat and with the rain we've had. Then you could maybe bring up a bucket of coal and chop some sticks. I'll get on with my knitting, I'm doing socks for Bert and Sam.'

Frank was thankful to have chores to do but before he began he asked after Belle's two brothers.

'Oh, Bert's in the Far East. He's a good lad and does write when he can and Sam's doing his training down south. He's just eighteen and joined up after his birthday. He's getting leave soon, it'll be good to see him.'

So Frank got out the old lawnmower and was soon pacing up and down the green between the clothes poles and enjoying the fresh air and exercise. He had changed into a pair of civilian trousers and a short sleeved shirt and felt as though the war was far away — certainly not here in Montrose in this back garden of the Davis's which was shared with several neighbours. Once the grass was cut to his satisfaction, he sat with Mrs Davis on a low wall and they sipped the glasses of lemonade she had thoughtfully brought out.

'It's good to have you here, Frank,' she said, then looked keenly at him. 'But what about your ain folk? Won't your Mam and Dad be looking for you going to see them?'

'Oh, aye, they surely will. But, you know, when there's ten of you and four of them are nearby to Mam and Dad, they don't fret too much. I'll go next time I get leave though, don't worry. And, once I've spoken to Belle this weekend, I'd like to take her to meet them.'

'Oh laddie, that would be fine. But, ca canny like, she's a good lass but took it badly the way Jim treated her. Give her a bit of time, won't you?'

'Time? Oh Mrs Davis, I certainly would if it wasn't for this darned war but who knows how much time any of us have?'

'Aye, I know lad. But ca canny just the same, won't you?'

Then she trotted off back up the stairs with the empty tumblers leaving Frank wondering just how much time Belle would need. If he had his way, they'd be wed next week but, yet, he knew Mrs Davis was right and he'd have to 'ca canny.'

Then he set to the other tasks of taking in the coal and chopping sticks after which he had a wash at the kitchen sink while Belle's Mum hung out some dish-towels and smalls she'd washed earlier at the same sink.

Soon though, Mr Davis and Belle were home, they had their salad tea followed by bread and jam and a cup of tea, then Belle went through to her bedroom. This was through from the front room with the budgie where they had sat the last time he had visited and she shared the bedroom with Elsie when she was on leave. Her parents' room was through from the kitchen cum living room and their two sons slept upstairs in the attic rooms. There was an outside, whitewashed lavatory shared with a neighbour and they counted themselves blessed compared to some folk where whole families shared two rooms.

Belle returned wearing a cotton summer dress in a fresh green colour with a dropped waistline, cap sleeves and sweetheart neckline. Her cream coloured, buckled court shoes completed the outfit and Frank was a proud man as he escourted her on their walk round the Traill Drive.

'So, eh, it's all off with you and Jim, eh Belle?' said Frank suddenly feeling awkward and tongue-tied.

Belle looked down and nodded slowly.

'Yes, I found he wasn't the man I thought he was. Well, you know the story — Elsie told you, didn't she?'

'Yes, she did that. If I could get hold of him, I'd choke him for hurting you.'

Belle stopped and they faced each other. Putting her hand on his arm, she said quietly:

'No, Frank, it's over. Let's forget it. I just want to put it behind me as a bad experience. I've learned from it not to be so trusting.'

'But Belle, you trust me, don't you? I would never hurt you.' Then throwing caution to the wind, he stumbled on. 'I love you, lass. I want to marry you. Be with you for the rest of my life.'

Belle reached up and put a finger to his lips.

'Please Frank, hush. It's too soon. Let's just enjoy each other's company. Be friends for now.'

It took all Frank's willpower to hold himself back but he remembered Mrs Davis's words and, taking on a jovial countenance he agreed that, sure, it was too soon, they'd just be friends for now. He went on,

'Come on, let's have a paddle in the

sea, then an ice-cream from the kiosk and sit and watch the sea-gulls.'

Belle realised how he must be feeling but joined in the pretended jollity and they ended up having fun splashing about at the edge of the breakers, drying their feet in the sand, then enjoying a cone up in the balcony of the Pavillion where he had been back in March with Elsie, Joe and Freda. Only five months ago, yet, to Frank, it seemed an eternity.

He stood slightly behind Belle as they looked over the links and golf-course to the north, and he admired the way her dark, wavy hair came down onto her shoulders, and her gentle curves and trim ankles. It was agony being with her and not being able to hold her, to kiss her, to . . . . Then she turned and looked up at him and her green eyes were trusting, were full of the love he felt for her and he knew it would be alright — he just had to be patient.

So the weekend passed and then, once again, he was back at Chester full of the bitter-sweet pain of loving and being loved but not having that love fulfilled. For a week or so, he and Joe spent their time off going into Chester and having just a bit too much to drink. When he could stand it no longer, he wrote to Belle and asked her to become engaged to him, but his heart sank at her reply.

Dear Frank,

Thank you for your lovely letter. As to your question about getting engaged, oh Frank, can you wait just a wee while longer? Montrose is still full of the gossip of my breaking it off with Jim. I want to be really sure I know what I'm doing this time. Hoping you're not working too hard. I'm looking forward to seeing you again.

Loving thoughts,
Belle.

On Frank's next leave, therefore, he went right up north to his folks in Banff and had a heart-to-heart talk with his Dad. Old Mr Pirie had been in an accident with a runaway horse when he'd worked on a farm and the resulting injuries had left him crippled. His wife, nothing daunted, had taken over a large house in Banff and ran it as a thriving boarding-house and tea-rooms.

Sitting outside one day of Frank's leave, his Dad, in between puffs on his pipe said,

'Frank, lad, women can be funny creatures. You push too hard and she'll run from you. Cool it a bit and she'll run to you. Take it from me, you'll find it's true.'

So Frank went back to Chester determined to take his Dad's advice. If he wrote at all he'd be casual and not come over too keen. He just hoped it would work.

8

Once Frank got back to the aerodrome, however, and had a chance to think it over, he changed tack. First, he thought about what Joe and Elsie had advised — 'go for it', then his Dad saying to stand back and play it cool. He made up his own mind though — to be true to his heart and what was in his character. So he wrote to Belle telling her he still loved her and would wait until she was ready, that he wouldn't write again until she replied in her own time. He added that he would stay true to her unless she made it clear that there was no hope for him.

A couple of weeks later, he and Joe were busy cleaning and maintaining the planes which had come back from sorties. It was now the beginning of September in the year 1940 and Frank was beginning to be despondent.

'Still no letter, pal?' asked Joe sympathetically.

'No, not a word. Mrs Davis's last week was the last I heard from any of them. She didn't give any real news, just saying that Mr Davis and Belle were still working away and that Belle stayed in most evenings. At least she's not courting anyone else.'

'Aye, well, women can be funny creatures. Look, come out with the lads tonight, we're going into Chester for a drink and there's a dance on. You can't mope about here forever.'

'Well I might just do that. I'm not getting involved with anyone though and by the sound of it, Belle's feeling as bad back in Montrose. It's as well we've plenty to keep us occupied and at least we're not flying these planes. Once we're sent abroad, we'll see plenty action then.'

So the two men carried on working then, as usual, Frank went off to see if there was anything in the mail for him. There was — a letter from his Mother and, although it was good to hear from her, he sighed with a heavy heart — still nothing from Belle. The chap with the mail walked on, then turned.

'Oh, sorry, Frank, I never noticed — here's another letter. Whoever it's from hasn't much to say — it's so thin — anyway better than nothing, eh pal?'

Frank looked down at the envelope and his spirits rose momentarily — yes, it was Belle's writing but what was the letter to say? Eagerly he went into his billet where one or two of the other men were doing various chores. Some of them, like himself, were opening their precious mail. He sat down on his bunk, put his Mother's letter aside for the minute and turned Belle's over in his hand. The letter must, indeed, be short, the envelope was so thin. Then, slitting it open, he took out the single sheet of paper.

Dear Frank, (he read)
What a fool I have been, keeping you waiting. I've missed you and am

miserable without you. I realise you're not like Jim and I just want to say that, when you are next on leave, if you still care for me, come to Montrose and we can get engaged. If people talk, let them. This war has made us all realise that we have to hang on to happiness when we can and I'm happy when I'm with you.

Yours lovingly,

Belle.

He read it again and again then let out a whoop. The other men looked up and grinned — obviously good news for one of them then. He ran outside to tell Joe, who was pleased for his friend who so much deserved a break.

'You'll still be coming out tonight, though?' he asked.

'No, lad. I'm replying to Belle right away after tea and I'll write to Mother too, with the news. Oh, Joe, I'm that happy I could burst. I'll away and read Mother's letter then we'll get on with the work although my head's in the clouds and I have to keep my feet on the ground. When do you think I'll get leave?'

'You can only ask, pal. Read your Mum's letter then see the officer. Even if you just get a weekend pass and spend some of it travelling, it'll be worth it, eh?'

So Frank read his Mother's letter which had all about how his brothers and sisters were faring and how the tearooms and boarding-house were aye busy. She ended by asking if there was any news of his 'bonny lass' which made him smile. Yes, he was one lucky lad.

He had to wait two whole weeks though before he could travel up to Montrose and then only for three days. He couldn't wait but it was to be a special weekend when he would be buying a ring for Belle, a symbol of their love. He'd written both to Belle and his own Mum but also to Belle's parents and they'd replied saying they were happy for the young couple to be engaged and that he could stay, once again, with their neighbours.

The two weeks passed and he set off. By the time he arrived in Montrose, it was after tea-time but he'd managed to get a pie and cup of tea at one of the stations they'd stopped at. Stepping off the train, he felt a bit nervous but then, there she was, smiling and holding out her arms. They hugged and hugged and he felt like he was in heaven. Then, hand in hand, with his bag slung over his shoulder, they made their way to Belle's home where a warm welcome awaited them. The four of them talked until they began to be sleepy and Mrs Davis reminded Belle that she was to be working the next day.

'Aye, Mam, but only in the morning. I've the afternoon off and Frank and I can choose the ring. Dunnett's have some fine ones.' Then colouring, she added shyly. 'I've been having a look in the window.'

They all had a chuckle at this, then Frank made his way downstairs to Mrs

Thomson where he would be sleeping. He thought he wouldn't sleep a wink but, to his surprise, he must have dozed off immediately and the first thing he knew it was morning and he heard Belle's footsteps on the stairs outside as she made to go off to work. Hastily he got up and dressed then went through to where Mrs Thomson was making bacon and egg for his breakfast.

'Just thought I'd give you a good breakfast, son,' she said kindly. 'I've a brother has a farm outside Montrose and I got a couple of eggs from him. I believe it's to be a special day for you.'

'Aye, it is that,' he said happily. 'I thought this day would never come. Thanks for giving me one of your precious eggs, they're a bit like hen's teeth, eh?' They chuckled then he added more seriously, 'Will there be much talk about Belle getting engaged so soon after breaking it off with Jim, do you suppose?'

'Ach, laddie, it'll be a seven day wonder if there is. Folk are too anxious about their own laddies and lassies going off to war to fash ower much about that. Now come on, get stuck in. I've done you a bit fried bread as well. Is that okay.'

'You're too good to me, Mrs Thomson. I won't forget it and you can dance at Belle and I's wedding.'

'That's good enough for me, lad. A bit of jollity amidst all this upheaval Hitler's caused in our lives. Have you things to do this morning?'

Frank stopped chewing to tell her that he hoped to cut their shared green at the back just as he'd done two months previously. After seeing the Davis's of course.

'Then I'll be washing and shaving to be presentable for my young lady,' he added with a twinkle in his eye. 'We'll maybe have a wee dram to celebrate tonight.'

True to his promise, he did cut the grass and tidy the edges then fetched in the coal, chopped sticks and generally made himself useful. After washing and shaving at the Davis's sink, he sat down to read the Dundee Courier which most local people bought each day. Soon though, Belle was home and they all had dinner together before Belle changed into the grey suit which he remembered she had worn that day back in March when he had discovered she was Elsie's sister.

Soon they were ready and set off up to Dunnett's, the jeweller in the High Street near to where Belle worked. Mr Dunnett was patient and kind and brought out two trays of rings which he felt might be right for their choice and for within Frank's price range.

Belle deliberated for a while, delighting in trying on first one ring then another but finally deciding on a diamond setting with two smaller stones at each side of a larger one. Frank was pleased she hadn't gone for too expensive a one, he was a canny Scot although he could be generous when it was needed.

The jeweller put the ring on a velvet

pad in a brown box which made a satisfactory clunk when it closed. He then put it in a small bag and handed it over with his congratulations. Frank put it in his pocket until they decided where and when he put in on her finger.

'I've already decided that,' she said. 'I thought as Mam and Dad have said we can sit in the front room this evening and have a drink to celebrate, we could then be on our own for a while. I'd like to get engaged then.'

'That's fine by me,' agreed Frank. 'Now, how about a stroll round to the sea front, it's not a bad day.'

It was, indeed a fine enough day with just a wee breeze, but the sun was bravely trying to shine and the happy couple wouldn't have noticed much anyway wrapped up as they were in themselves as they strolled along. They knew they would always cherish this day.

Arriving back at Carnegie Street, Mr and Mrs Davis admired the ring which they declared was 'just right', then

Frank was despatched up to the nearby fish 'n' chip shop for their tea. There was much hilarity as they ate them from the newspaper they were wrapped up in and said they always tasted better that way. After carefully putting the vinegar-saturated paper into the fire when they had eaten, they then enjoyed a cup of tea and scones.

'My, that was braw,' said Mr Davis as he and Frank settled to listen to a military band playing on the radio while the two women washed up the cups.

'Now, we'll awa through the house,' said Mrs Davis. 'We've the fire going through there and a wee drink set out for us.'

So through to the front room they went where Billy the budgie whistled chirpily at having company. He was often brought through to the cosier kitchen but only when Mrs Davis's bronchitis wasn't too bad as his feathers irritated her breathing.

On a small table was a half bottle of whisky, a bottle of sherry and a soda siphon. The fire was burning brightly and, as Belle's parents took the two easy chairs, Frank was delighted to sit with Belle on the sofa.

'We'll have a wee drink and perhaps Belle will give us a tune on the piano, then we'll leave you to yourselves for Frank to give you the ring, Belle,' said Mrs Davis.

So Belle's Dad poured the drinks and the older couple wished them every happiness. Then Belle sat down on the piano stool and played 'Some Enchanted Evening' once again. Then she played 'Greensleeves' and they all joined in the singing of this tune. Mr and Mrs Davis then left them saying to Frank not to be late in going downstairs as they all had to be up for church in the morning. The young couple were amused to see they took the drink away with them when they left the room, saying their goodnights.

'Ah, Belle, you've made me so happy,' said Frank huskily and he pulled her gently up off the sofa. Taking her in his arms, he kissed her a bit awkwardly as he wasn't very experienced with women, then, gaining confidence, their feelings gave way to passion like neither of them had known before. Using all his self-control, he drew away and reached into his pocket for the box containing the ring.

'Will you marry me?' he asked, looking longingly into her eyes and she nodded and smiled up at him. After slipping the ring onto the third finger of her left hand, they then kissed again and sat down on the sofa with Frank's arm still round her.

'Oh, Belle, you're doing crazy things to me. I can hardly wait until we're married.'

She pulled a bit apart and they made small talk about when next he would be on leave and when they might think about setting the date. Then Frank pulled her into his arms once more and found himself placing his hand on her knee. She stiffened a little and, when he explored further, she reached down and put her hand on his, stopping him.

'No, Frank, I don't want it to be like that. Mam and Dad trust us here and anyway I want to wait until we are married.'

Strangely enough Frank was glad and relieved. He'd only been trying her and now knew she was, indeed, the kind of girl he had always longed for.

Shortly afterwards he took his leave and went downstairs and, this time, in bed, he lay awake for a long while thanking God he'd been blessed with a lass like Belle who he just wanted to spend the rest of his life with.

9

After his lovely weekend in Montrose, Frank was quite happy to be back in Chester, knowing that he and Belle were promised to each other and that she was wearing his ring. The weeks passed with letters to-ing and fro-ing between them. It was a bright breezy day in October when the post brought yet another letter from his beloved. Frank took it to his billet, sat down on his bunk and eagerly tore open the envelope.

Dearest Frank, (he read)
Oh my sweetheart, I am so sorry and so upset, I don't know how to tell you. (Frank's heart sank, wondering what had happened. Was she to be calling it off?)
Last night (the letter continued) I washed up the supper dishes and, as

usual, put my ring on the mantelpiece for safety but forgot to put it back on before going to bed. When I looked for it this morning it wasn't there. Then Dad found it when cleaning out the ashes. Oh Frank, it is all burnt, almost half of it destroyed. I am heartbroken. The remaining half of it is in its box but I can't ever wear it again.

My love, I won't blame you if you are angry. Mum and Dad are so sorry also and we don't know how it happened but they said to write and tell you right away. I won't expect another ring. Please forgive me.

Your loving,
Belle.

Frank sat stunned for a minute then did, indeed feel mounting anger. How could she be so careless? She'd only had the ring for a month. How could he trust her with anything again? The thoughts went round and round in his head until finally, he realised he'd have to get back to work. The jeep he'd been stripping and cleaning had never had such a shine before as he gradually worked out his anger on it. Anyone passing and calling out to him got short shift until he realised he wasn't doing any good blaming Belle. After all, however it fell off the mantelpiece into the fire, it wasn't necessarily her fault and it had most certainly been accidental.

Over their meal later, he told Joe about it and his dear chum understood and said laughingly,

'It looks like the sooner you two are married the better, so you can keep an eye on her, eh?'

Frank slapped his hand on the table.

'You're right, pal. I'll write tonight and suggest she sets a date for the wedding. I do forgive her but there's to be no other engagement ring. The only other ring she'll get is a wedding band. Oh, Joe, if I didn't love her so much, but I do and I should just be grateful she's still my lass and — soon to be my wife.'

So he wrote back to Belle saying just that — that she was forgiven, once his anger had cooled, that there would be no other replacement ring and would she like to set the date for their wedding as soon as possible?

Belle was relieved she was forgiven, though it wasn't really her fault and although she'd never have another engagement ring, she understood and accepted it. After seeing their minister at St Luke's church, they agreed on 1st January, 1941 for the day of their wedding. Elsie would be home and would be bridesmaid and, on finding that none of Frank's brothers could be there, they asked his sister Gladys's sweetheart, George, to be best man. As it was a holiday, being New Year's day, they decided to be wed in the nearby Park Hotel and that it would be a quiet affair with only Belle's parents, Elsie and Joe, Gladys and George, Belle's pal, Nan and her parents, Mr and Mrs Cook, who they would stay their first night with and their neighbour, Mrs

Thomson. They were just sorry that Frank's parents couldn't manage the journey and Belle's brothers couldn't get leave.

Belle managed to get a smart lilac suit and matching hat from Helen Carnegie's where Elsie had worked before the war and it was a happy band who set off for the Park Hotel on the day.

Frank, George and Joe set off first to wait for the bridal party. Then a quietly excited Belle along with Elsie and Mr and Mrs Davis, travelled the short distance in a taxi. After meeting up with the others, Mr Davis took Belle's arm in his and walked her to where Frank and George stood waiting. Frank was smart in his uniform and his eyes shone with happiness at the sight of his radiant bride at his side

They took their vows solemnly, said 'I do' at the appropriate time, exchanged rings and, after kissing lovingly, were congratulated by everyone. There was much merriment as they enjoyed their meal of scotch broth, boiled ham, potatoes and vegetables followed by sherry trifle and a celebratory drink.

Much later, the happy couple walked with Mr and Mrs Cook to the older couple's home at the other end of town.

'Thank you so much for having us to stay the night,' said Belle shyly as they sat sipping tea and enjoying home-baked cakes and biscuits by the fireside.

'Ach lassie, it's a pleasure to hae you,' said Mrs Cook. 'When Nan said you couldn't get away on honeymoon because of the time of year and Frank's short leave, we thought you could at least have a change of abode for the nicht.'

The two men sat chatting afterwards while Belle and Mrs Cook washed up the dishes. Then it was bedtime and Mrs Cook showed them through to the bedroom which was normally kept for their daughter, Nan. First though they each went in turn to the outside lavatory to relieve themselves.

Alone at last in the bedroom, neither of them having had much experience with the opposite sex before, they scuttered around, unpacking their night things before starting to undress. The room had been heated by a paraffin heater and lit by a gas-mantle but Belle shivered a little in anticipation of what lay ahead.

Frank was undressed first and was into his pyjama bottoms and sitting up in bed with a grin on his face, while Belle brushed her hair at the dressing-table mirror. Feeling a bit discomfited, she too began to undress, annoyed at his apparent amusement. Once into her nightie, she slipped under the covers beside him and felt better as his arms came round her.

'Oh, lass,' he said. 'You don't know how I've longed for this moment.'

'Me too, Frank. Be gentle with me, won't you? I've never . . . well never . . . before.'

'Nor me,' Frank admitted. 'Oh I'm just glad it's the first time for both of us.'

Then, as their feelings carried them

away, they were just getting into the rhythm of it all when they heard a jingling, jangling noise.

'What on earth,' exclaimed Frank. Then, as they carried on, so did the noise.

'That Nan,' said Belle. 'I'll kill her.'

'What is it?' asked Frank mystified.

'The besom's gone and tied bells to the springs of the bed.'

Groaning, Frank tried to fulfil their marriage for the third time but it was no use and he rolled off her in dismay. Then the humour of the situation hit them and Frank joined in Belle's chuckling until the two of them were suffused in laughter. Finally overcome with emotion and tiredness, they held hands and slept, knowing they had the rest of their lives together.

10

Their marriage was well and truly consummated the following night in Belle's bed which she usually shared with Elsie when she was on leave. Then they had the Monday together before, early on Tuesday morning, Frank had to take the train back down south once again. Belle also had to get back to her work in the newsagents but had time to go with Frank to the station first.

'Oh Frank, I wish you didn't have to go so soon,' said Belle as they clung to each other.

'I know, lass. I feel the same but oh, it's been wonderful, you're wonderful. I can't believe you're my wife when, at this time last year I didn't even know you. I just used to watch you pass as I stood up closes in the High Street.'

'And I didn't know you were there and I was engaged to someone else. I'm glad I met you though and . . . . oh, here's the train — oh Frank.'

Frank kissed her soundly as the train came hissing and tooting into the station. Giving each other one final hug, he got in, the door was shut behind him but he pulled down the window and leant out to grip her hands.

'Write soon,' they both said in unison then, as the train tooted again, the porter shouted:

'All aboard' and waved his flag. It was off and Belle ran a little way alongside then they waved and waved to each other until the train was out of sight.

Once back at Chester, the other men, including Joe ribbed him mercilessly, then he settled down to the monotonous work of maintaining the trucks, jeeps and planes all the while wishing he was with Belle.

Then, after a couple more visits to Montrose on leave they had a memorable visit up north to Banff for Belle to meet his folks. They liked each other on sight. Belle loved the upright, indomitable woman his Mother was as she worked hard to keep the boarding-house and tearoom going. She also took to Frank's likable Father with his moustache and beard and his twinkling eyes which showed his sense of humour was never far away. They, in turn, were happy with Frank's lovely new wife with her slim figure and dark hair and whose gentle, kind nature was evident.

Soon, it was the summer of 1941 and, one day Belle arrived home from work to find a letter from Frank. This was one of many but she eagerly tore open the envelope and began to read it.

'Oh Mam,' she gasped, 'listen to this.' She began to read it aloud.

'Dearest Wife,' — he loves starting with that,' she said laughing, then went on,

'It was so good taking you to meet Mother and Dad and they loved you as I knew they would. Now dear, I have a bit of news for you, we are being moved on. We leave in two days to travel to a place called Bridgend in South Wales. It is in the county of Glamorgan which is said to be very picturesque. The thing is, we are getting our wives to stay with us at various homes in the village and, oh my darling, it would be so good if you could come. I understand you'll have to get a replacement at your work but pray that, before long, you can make the journey there. I'll find out the different stations where you'll have to change and let you know. To have you beside me every night, your . . . ' Her voice trailed off and she looked at her Mum, a bit embarrassed.

'It's alright, Belle. I don't need to know all the letter,' said Mrs Davis chuckling. 'Some things are just between man and wife. But, oh lass, you will go, won't you? It's so good Frank's not having to go abroad — not yet anyway. You should be together while you can.'

Belle looked thoughtful.

'Yes Mam. Of course I want to go. But what if I'm still away in the winter and you take ill? How will you cope?'

'Ach, lassie. I've your Dad, and Elsie gets home now and then and the neighbours are good. No, you should be with your man. Now, come on, have your dinner before it spoils and you can tell your boss this afternoon. He'll have to advertise your job. It'll be filled easily enough by some lassie not wanting to go into the Mill. And you'll have news of your own to tell Frank when you see him, will you no'?'

Belle did indeed have news to tell Frank and, when all the plans were quickly made and she had said a tearful goodbye to her parents, she made the long journey to the heart of Wales. Frank was at the bus-stop to meet her and, after loving greetings, took her to meet the family whose home they would be staying in.

'Meet Mr and Mrs Owen, love. This is my wife, Belle,' he said and Mr Owen, a large, bluff elderly man boomed out.

'Dav-vid, just call me Dav-vid and

this is Bronwen. Now came away and we'll haff our meal.'

Belle immediately felt at home with the Owens but couldn't wait to see Frank on his own. Later, after helping clear up, the young couple strolled along the village street happy to be together. They stopped by a stile and hugged and kissed oblivious of any passers-by.

'Frank,' said Belle lovingly, 'can you sing?'

'Sing?' queried Frank, bewildered. 'About as well as I can dance — but why are you asking?'

'Well, do you think, if we had a son or a daughter, they'd be able to sing?'

'Eh, Belle, I think the long journey has gone to your head. Perhaps we'll have an early night.'

Belle laughed delightedly.

'But Frank, they say all Welshmen can sing and I thought if our child were born here, well . . . .'

Frank looked down at her stunned, then whispered,

'Our child — you mean?' Then, as she nodded he let out a whoop. 'Oh lass, I didn't think I could get much happier. Come here.'

And so it was. On February 10th, 1942, a precious little dark haired, brown eyed son was born to them in Bridgend hospital with bombs dropping all around. He was named Andrew George David Pirie with the David included because Mr Owen insisted on it and they were happy to oblige.

The next months were happy ones with Frank dividing his time between the work at the aerodrome and sharing and caring for his wife and son. They decided to go home to Montrose for the christening and, although the train journey was awkward with Belle breast-feeding the baby and trying to get privacy to do so, they eventually arrived.

Mr and Mrs Davis were overjoyed to see them and Belle's Mum immediately took the shawl-wrapped bundle into her arms and murmured:

'My first grandchild.'

Then it was all hustle and bustle as they set up the borrowed cot and, after catching up on all the news, they settled down for the night.

The christening went well with baby Andrew just giving a wee greet as the water was sprinkled on his head. Rev Birkbeck was a lovely man and the proud parents remembered when he'd married them just over a year before.

Soon though, it was time for them to return to Wales and, once again, there were tearful goodbyes.

The months passed and Andrew grew steadily sturdier and stronger. Soon he was a year old and was already beginning to toddle and say a few words.

Not long after, Frank came bursting into the Owens' living-room one day. Mrs Owen was sitting knitting, David was brushing his shoes and Belle was playing 'Peek-a-bo' with Andrew. They all looked up, startled.

'We're getting moved on,' said Frank.

'To Bearley, in England.'

'Bearley?' questioned Belle.

'Yes, it's near Stratford-on-Avon.'

'When?' asked Belle anxiously.

'In three days. Oh Belle, you'll have to come later with Andy once I've found a home for you.'

'Ba, and we'll miss you,' said David. They all agreed that indeed they would miss each other.

So Frank once again moved out with his company leaving Belle to pack up and follow when he wrote to say he'd found a couple of rooms for them in the home of an elderly bachelor.

It was an exhausted Belle with a grizzly Andrew who finally arrived at the village of Bearley after several changes of trains and buses. Belle's heart sank further when she met the elderly man, Mr Tom Duncan, who stared at her from under his bushy eyebrows. All at once she felt a sense of foreboding and just wished she was safely home with her parents or even back in Wales with the Owens.

11

Over the next few months, Frank began to see subtle changes in Belle. She was still loving towards him, yet seemed on edge and was losing weight. He liked working away at the base at Bearley, but began more and more to sense a tense atmosphere in Tom Duncan's home. One night, lying side by side in bed with Belle, he heard her give a stifled sob.

'Belle, darling, whatever's the matter? Are you well enough?' he asked anxiously. Belle tensed then turned towards him.

'Oh, Frank, I didn't want to worry you but, well, I just don't like living here. It's old Tom . . . .' her voice trailed away.

'Tom? What's he done — he hasn't laid a hand on you has he?'

'No, no, nothing like that. It's just

that he's always staring at me and follows me around, hardly speaking, with a leering grin on his face. And, today, wee Andy was playing with his toy trucks at the fireside and I caught Tom poking him with his walking-stick. Andy started to greet and I took him for a long walk in his pram. I often do that just to get away from the house.'

'Oh, Belle, my love, why didn't you tell me before? I realised he's a taciturn old man but I had no idea he was bothering you. Look, I'll ask the lads tomorrow, see if they know of anyone else who will take us in. It'll be alright, you'll see. And maybe in another house, we'll have more privacy at night. These walls are paper thin and with the old man just through there and us sharing a room with Andy, well . . . . you know.'

'I know, Frank.' Belle gave a relieved giggle. 'If we could find another place, oh it would be so good. I just didn't want to worry you. I could put up with a lot myself but don't want it to affect Andy or for our marriage to suffer. I should have known you would understand. Thank you love.'

Frank kissed and cuddled her and they made love as quietly as they could without disturbing Andy or the old man. It was the first time for a few weeks and the tension which had built up just ebbed away in the aftermath of their lovemaking.

The next morning things looked so much brighter and, to his further relief, Frank found that a family in the village had a spare room to let out as their previous lodger, another airman, had moved on.

Frank hurried home at lunchtime and said to Belle to get wee Andy ready to go out as he had a surprise for her. They walked to the other side of the village pushing the pram with Andy chattering away in his baby talk and pointing at birds, trees and flowers as they strode along.

'It's just one room in this family's home, Belle, and we'll have to share a bathroom and kitchen with the family but they sound a nice couple. They have two young daughters of their own so that'll be company for Andy.'

'Oh Frank, I won't mind sharing and it'll be so good having another woman to talk to again. It's been a lonely, frustrating few months. Oh, is this the house?'

Frank had stopped at a garden gate and they looked up at the two-storey, detached building, quite impressed and delighted.

'Oh and Frank, it has a garden for the bairns to play in. It's coming up to the winter months but it will still be good just to have the extra space. I do hope they can take us.'

Mr and Mrs Parsons, or Mary and Les as they asked to be called, along with their children, Doreen and Margaret, were indeed able to have them stay and, for the first time since coming to Bearley, Belle felt happy and able to relax.

They soon settled into a routine with the two women sharing the chores and seeing to the wee ones and Frank helping out where he could.

'Brr, it's chilly tonight,' he said coming into the house with a bundle of logs for the fire.

'Oh, you're such a help, Frank. Les isn't so able with having a bad chest. He's never got over having to have a desk job in the army but it's what suits him best when all is said and done. He'd never have been able to handle a truck or a rifle. Don't let on I told you that, though.' Mary's eyes twinkled kindly behind her spectacles. Although her children were young, she was nearly forty and often told Belle and Frank that she thought she'd never meet 'Mr Right'. Then, when she was thirty-three, she had met Les and, after a whirlwind romance, they had wed and along came the children, before, as she put it, 'she had time to draw breath'.

Both families got on well and, although Les was often away at camp, when he was home, they would all muck in quite happily.

Soon it was Andy's second birthday and they had a wee tea-party for him. They all sat round the table eating sandwiches and home-baking. There was even a birthday cake and, though it was made with dried egg, they all declared it delicious.

That night, Belle and Frank lay in each others' arms after a particularly blessed time of loving.

'Oh, Frank, I'm so happy. Andy's settled down here so well and, though the girls and him sometimes squabble, it's nothing serious and they're soon the best of pals again. We won't have to move to another place, will we? Now that he's two it's maybe not a good idea us all sharing a bedroom. Not that I mind but he's just getting so knowing . . . . you know?'

Frank laughed softly.

'Aye, indeed. But we're fine here just now. And who knows when we might be moved away from Bearley altogether? Let's just make the most of our time here.'

Frank didn't know just how prophetic his words were. Soon it was June, 1944 and Belle suspected she was expecting another child. She planned to tell Frank in bed that night but, first, when he came in, he sat down at the table with a thump and looked a bit shocked.

Belle and Mary glanced at each other wonderingly and the children, sensing something was up, stopped their play and stared solemnly at the adults.

'Frank,' said Belle, putting a hand on his shoulder. 'Is everything okay?'

Frank roused himself.

'I wondered how long we would get away with it. But the time's come. We're being sent abroad.'

There was silence then the two women spoke at once.

'Abroad — where, when?'

'I think it will be France or Belgium to begin with and well, we're moving out next week.'

Belle felt relieved that it wasn't the Far East or somewhere more sinister but then remembered her own news. What would happen now? Where would she and Andy go? There would be new airmen coming to the base and their room would surely be needed. Oh, just when everything was going so well.

That night she shared the news about the baby which, she had worked out, had been conceived on Andy's second birthday. Frank was delighted and yet sombre at the same time. He lay deep in thought for a while, then said quietly,

'I want you to go home Belle. Home to Montrose. Stay with your Mum and Dad. I'll feel better with you there and you can have the baby at 8 Carnegie Street. We'll write as often as we can and I'll come home when I can, if I can. Oh, Belle, I'm going to miss you so much.'

They held each other tight, too much was happening too soon but so long as they had each other, along with wee Andy and the expected baby, they'd come through it.

12

Frank's unit moved out just as he had said. They sailed from Dover to Calais and, as the white hills they knew about from one of the war-time songs gradually faded from sight, he and his fellow airmen wondered what lay ahead for them.

As it turned out, Frank's last year of war was a good one apart from his longing for Belle and wee Andy. He, besides driving trucks over France and Belgium, found himself doing his stint as cook in the mess kitchens and even arranging entertainment for the men. By this time he was promoted to a sergeant with three stripes on his sleeve.

'Frank seems to be enjoying himself,' said Belle to her Mum after reading one of his letters. 'He says they had Ann Shelton, the singer who sings for the forces, at their unit. I think he's having a better time than he had over here.'

'Oh well, lass, so long as he's safe. I'm sure they're just making the most of it. Let's hope it's all over soon.'

'Aye Mam, I hope so. I wonder what'll come first, this baby or the end of the war.'

'We'll ken soon enough. Now stop ironing and sit down for a while, you'll get swollen ankles.'

So Belle and her Mum enjoyed a welcome cup of tea while Andy, now two and a half years old, played at their feet.

Soon it was the end of October and, one morning, Belle felt the first pangs of childbirth hit her as she knelt to clear the ashes from the fireplace.

'Ooh Mam, I think it's the baby starting. Oh help me up, I feel so big and clumsy.'

Just then her waters broke and Mrs Davis struggled to help Belle to her feet and into an armchair.

'Dinna worry lass, just sit there. I'll

run downstairs for Mrs Thomson and we'll send for the midwife.'

'No, not yet Mam. Get Mrs Thomson but Mrs Skinner, the midwife can wait a whilie yet.'

So Mrs Thomson helped clean up the mess of the waters and the three women sat together drinking tea and chatting, hoping to take Belle's mind off the pains when they came. They had lit the fire and it gave off a cheery warmth. Wee Andy had been through in the other room when Belle's waters broke and was now looking at a storybook and seemed oblivious to what was going on round about him.

The day wore on and there was still no sign of the bairn making his or her appearance. At tea-time Mr Davis returned from work, had a quick tea then said he'd take Andy out for a walk. Belle's brother, Sam, was home on leave and he and his fiancée, Yvonne, also looked in, had a bite to eat, then said they too would have a walk as still nothing much was happening with Belle, apart from pains coming and going.

'Right, let's get this wee lad to bed,' said Mrs Davis after her husband and grandson returned from their walk.

'No going to bed,' said Andy, his bottom lip pouting. 'Stay here wif Mummy.'

'Come on, laddie,' said his granddad. 'I'll tell you a wee story and, in the morning you'll have a baby brother or sister.'

Andy pondered at this, looking up at his granddad with big trusting brown eyes.

'Want a wee bruvver. Will he play wif my ball wif me?'

'We'll see. Now, come on and I'll read you a story.'

So Andy was put to bed and, not long after, Sam and Yvonne returned home.

'Michty Belle, have you no' had the bairn yet?' said Yvonne incredulously.

Mrs Davis looked anxious.

'Let's get you through to the front room, Belle. The double bed there is all ready.'

Belle, who was pale and exhausted, readily agreed and Mrs Skinner, the elderly midwife was sent for. While the womenfolk were in the other room seeing to Belle, Mr Davis and Sam sat and talked about football, the war, the railway and anything else they could think of to take their minds off the goings on through in the other room.

Midnight came and went and Yvonne and Sam were sitting side by side on the sofa getting sleepier and sleepier. Yvonne was determined to be there when the baby was born even though she had her work at the Co-op that day. 'I think I'll hap you two up with a blanket,' said Mrs Davis kindly and did so, tucking them in cosily together knowing there would be no hanky-panky.

Mrs Thomson and Mrs Skinner were meanwhile still there for Belle while Mrs Davis went back and forth making cups of tea for everyone. It was 5 o'clock on the morning of 30th

October, 1944, before they heard the faint wails of the new-born baby and they all sent up a fervent prayer of thanks.

'It's a lass, a bonnie wee lass,' said Mrs Davis coming through and wiping away a tear. 'Belle's gie tired but they're both okay. Now we'll a' maybe get some sleep.'

It was a bewildered little boy who was awakened later that morning to be told he had a wee sister.

'Don't want a wee sister,' he scowled and promptly lay down and thumped his feet up and down on the floor.

This jealousy went on for some time but, every time Elsie returned from England, she took baby Alison Susan Pirie, as she had been christened, out so much, that he soon began to settle down, knowing that there would still be times he had his Mum to himself.

Frank, meanwhile, was over the moon to have a baby daughter and his longing grew to be home with his wee family.

It wasn't until May 1945 that, at last, the war was over and there were many celebrations. For Frank, though, the worst part was yet to come.

'We've to pick up some of these poor lads who've been in concentration camps, Joe,' he said sadly to his old mate with whom he'd seen through the war. 'I feel ashamed we've had it so easy — who knows what horrors they've seen.'

Indeed it was devastating for the airmen to drive their trucks into Germany to pick up the emaciated men who had been interred. They were like walking skeletons and Frank felt sickened at how men could treat their fellow human beings. It was, indeed, the most heart-rending part of the whole war for him and he knew it would take much nursing and loving care to bring these poor souls back to even feeling human again.

Finally, though, he was on his way home and, as he stepped off the train at Montrose station once again, his rucksack slung over his shoulder, he felt tears in his eyes as he looked over at the tidal basin on one side with the sun glinting on the water and, to the east, the town's steeple still standing proudly.

No-one at 8 Carnegie Street knew exactly when he would be arriving but, he stood and tapped at the door then opened it and shouted 'Coo-ee anyone at home?'

He went through to the kitchen and the sight there warmed his heart. It was as though he had never been away. Mr and Mrs Davis sat at either side of the coal-fire which was burning brightly and they both rose and hugged him tightly.

'Oh, lad, it's so good to see you home. Belle's just feeding Alison. The wee lass has teeth now and she'll have to be weaned soon,' said Mrs Davis beaming up at her son-in-law who, although thinner, was as wholesome and handsome as ever. 'Belle, Belle, he's here lass.'

Then Belle came through buttoning

her blouse and the couple, who had been apart for over a year, came together in a joyful embrace.

'Oh, Frank, you're home at last,' she said with a sob. And they looked into each other's eyes and the love reflected there was stronger than ever.

Wee Andy came toddling through. He was three now and stood shyly, clutching his teddy. This man in uniform was familiar and they were telling him it was his Daddy back from the war. Frank got down on his haunches and looked into his son's eyes, as dark as his own.

'Hello, son,' said Frank lovingly. 'Have you a hug for your old Dad?'

After just a minute they bonded and Andy reached out with his teddy to Frank who picked his son up into the air, then they too hugged as the boy squealed his delight.

'Alison through here,' said Andy slowly. 'My wee sister. Ssh, she's sleeping.'

He was over his jealousy by now and

pulled Frank through to see his nine month old baby daughter for the first time. She was indeed, sleeping soundly but Frank couldn't help picking her up out of her cot and, after an indignant yelp, her eyes opened wide and she too gazed into her Daddy eyes. A big chuckle came from her throat and she reached out and clutched his nose. Her fair curls and big brown eyes bewitched him and his throat tightened with love.

As he held his 'wee Susie,' as he immediately started calling her, with Andy at his knee and Belle coming through and placing her hand on his shoulder, he thought of the emaciated men he had helped bring to safety. Never, he vowed, would his wife, son or daughter ever have to face such atrocities. He felt his baby's sturdy limbs and that of wee Andy's and a popular tune of the day Tea for Two, came into his mind.

'We will raise a family, a boy for you, a girl for me, can't you see how